no v

no visual scars

ANGELA HRYNIUK

POLESTAR
BOOK PUBLISHERS

no visual scars

Published by:
Polestar Press Ltd.
2758 Charles Street, Vancouver, B.C., V5K 3A7
and
6496 Youngs North Road, Winlaw, B.C., V0G 2J0

Distributed in Canada by:
Raincoast Book Distribution Ltd.
112 East Third Avenue, Vancouver, B.C., V5T 1C8

Some of these poems have been published in the chapbooks
...that night were painfully wept, tough love and *precious cargo*; or in the following journals: *Island, Zest, The Uniter, dandelion, Fireweed, Between You, Me and the Stars, JAG, Images, Swift Current, Transition* and *Contemporary Verse 2.*

Published with the assistance of the Canada Council
and the British Columbia Cultural Services Branch.

Cover art: An Argument Older Than Ourselves (detail) by Nancy Boyd
Author photo by Peter Timmermans
Cover design by Jim Brennan
Production and editing by Michelle Benjamin
Printed in Canada

Canadian Cataloguing in Publication Data
Hryniuk, Angela, 1963-
No visual scars
Poems.
ISBN 0-919591-78-7
I. Title.
PS8565.R96N6 1993   C811'.54   C93-091002-8
PR9199.3.H79N6 1993

Acknowledgements

Fred Wah and Daphne Marlatt — thank you for your poetry and teachings. For your encouragement, loving support and advice, thank you Christine, Ann, Betsy, Leonard, Liz, Jill, John and Jeannie. Bill, Judith, June, Phillip, Dianne, Jill, John, John, Keren, Cam and Susan — thank you all for bringing such wonderful children into my world and showing your courage and honesty in pregnancy. Many thanks Michelle at Polestar for your enthusiasm and expertise. And Stephen Fearing, who without fail was there for me, thanks.

for Stephen

…that night were painfully wept

no visual scars

portraits of pregnant women

...that night were painfully wept

desire bites

desire bites
like a vampire (I want to write)
but no
more like
the soft & strong brush of a butterfly
next to our cheek
where does the appetite hibernate
in our bodies
sometimes betray us
the unseen hunger
claws at us
the unexpected hurricane
turns its eye on us
the undertow of the wave
pulls us to our knees
& in the dawn
teeth marks left on our throat
(I thought I threw that metaphor away)
it ricochets
always
our actions follow us
whomever we're with
vampires & butterflies both always know
where the open window is

la luna *llena*

warm by light of the Mexican moon plop my tiny looks like
child's chair in wet sand between two wooden fishing boats rest
wait for tomorrow's crew Victor tells me they fish at night catch
the fish's attention don't fish tonight full moon too bright so
boats won't leave the sand sea roars to my right the wave turns its
lip up onto shore white froth sound of wind or heavy sheet of
rain in the distance then back again recedes. the tide came near
the tents last night full moon seduces water closer & closer teases
then retreats. fear the sister there is a powerful one she & I have
warm conversations when I travelled across the prairies this
summer her body full rich orange rust beckoned me to say only a
few words & I did oh I did. where I live now in the mountains
she & I no longer see one another as often although yes,
remember one night I sank deep inside a darkness dressed in
black skirt black blazer tall beige hat feather flowing out of it. she
guided me home kissed me into sleep the tears that night were
painfully wept I remember now sit on a rickety old chair built for
someone half my size can only be good for Mexican men, any of
the women I've seen are as wide as they're tall I lean back dream
about her & her strength

la luna llena *means full moon;* llena *also means pregnant.*

between two oceans

I say to you quickly after a night of
sipping wine I love you but awake
with the fear I've frightened you away
said things I might regret
if I were sober I couldn't be
in the same room as her & you
she's like a sister to me
you explained before the party but
mothers are possessive sisters aren't
I left the party alone you crawled
through my bedroom window my door
locked for the first time in a while
you stroked my face with your long
fingers as I pretended to sleep in the
morning you were gone

∽

we walk beside one another along winding railroad
tracks bend with the black Kootenay lake
full moon sparkles lights of Nelson
in the distance we stroll you tell me about
growing up in Ireland hiding
your talent in a boarding school room
guitar playing at 15 your history teacher knowing
there was more than your poor marks in class
until one day you pulled him aside & played
now here this side of the ocean
you skip years telling me the story
your hand in mine along the tracks
pick a spot behind an unlit warehouse to sit
you hopped trains from Minneapolis to Seattle
when you first arrived now we sit in total darkness
of each other getting to know the railroad tracks
afraid a train will come

〜

I'm spending time down by the railroad tracks
sit with rust stripes across the ass of my jeans
walk down from my house between the highway
& train whistle wakes me at night the house shakes
I felt alive in bed with you as it went along
the tracks in early grey mornings thinking of nights
with you at the docks fish truck
on its regular saturday stop little old man with a navy woolen cap
short stubby fingers nails bitten quickly handles fish
& money in one motion I pass by to watch the ducks
plunge in the lake afraid of me why is everyone afraid of me?
first night after the party we made our way
down the wind gusted off the lake your peajacket collar
turned up my *babushka* tight over my ears we snuggled
where the wind wouldn't catch us promising
to one another this would be a casual affair
solidify a friendship later you confide in me
in bed as I'm tucked into your body neither of us thought
it would go this far or be like this

5

love. well Dublin Bay boy, my dear man, is a strange & ever-
lasting that makes the world tick tock turn on its axis day after
night after day. & you & me & you are engaged in the tangled
net of the ageless word. but are we if we're aware of what really is?

℘

a storm brews outside the house
a grey wind picks up
clouds crawl in
along the mountain's edge
the maple trees jungle the house
swish against the window

the furniture in every room
sits silent
walls cleared of colourful woven rugs
drawers emptied of underwear & socks
even the clothesline is down
but half the house
is still
alive somehow

〜

I find remnants of you
lying around people's houses
I walk into Linda's
see a guitar
propped against the wallpapered wall
assume it's yours

I visit Michael
have a coffee & chat
out of the corner of my eye I see
a box of your clothes

slowly I walk home
along the water's edge
want something tangible
to remember you by
as I enter the bedroom
I notice on the floor
an ashtray with a butt
from your lips squished
by your thumb
buried in ashes
beside the bed

the blue '67 Valiant crosses my path
many times each day
I walk across Baker Street
see your car & look for your face
your body hunched over the wheel
but know we're between two oceans

∽

weeks pass
even months
& still
you're here
in my red heart
keeps moving
city after city
you too
never stand still
to stagnate to stammer to
stutter or shuffle no
always in motion
by plane by bike by foot by
& bye

∽

so is love as wide as arms will stretch out
around a redwood tree? the little stars
seen in front of the eyes the fizz of light
inside the gut at the mention of a name
where does the rational reasoning fit into
the remembered roses or spontaneous bubble baths
& wine no pin prickly pink feelings
they only surface with your body presence
standing naked in front of me thoughts drag on
in the mind carry on to the next letter or

yes flashes
not quite so alive
as before
more ethereal in dream
can put a hand through the image
your face
once the actual name is spoken
rainbows appear in my mouth
if it all blows up
in my face in my lap
my head in my hands

∽

I lie in bed
& hold myself again
this time I can't wait
for the return
this time is the last
for waiting

twist & turn the strings attached
to the words *I love you*
circulate through the body
in the mouth roll around
on the tip of blue lips
next to white clenched teeth tight
at night
in bed toss & turn
those words

no longer a black-tasting liquor
I sip
hard & quick scotch
goes to my head
after a night's work
the slow decay of my bones
I wonder how to stop
daily the ocean widens
across it's only 2,000 miles no?
the same distance
between Vancouver & Newfoundland
so what's the big deal
everyone loses a lover

∽

everyone loses a lover
everyone thinks it's a first
I'm prepared
like the prepared mustard
sits on a shelf at Safeway
waits to be picked
for a sandwich or a hamburger
waits to be taken off the shelf
to be useful
even if in the end
only the glass jar remains
the insides all used up
that's what mustard's for
flavour

I know you're here somewhere
on this round planet
circulates
the full moon rises
& falls
you see it too
from where I don't know
tonight
could be in Ireland
could already be back on Canadian soil
snuggle yet again
in a foreign bed
maybe the last night
in your childhood bed
only imagine where
the covers
what do they feel like?
feather quilt or a sheet & piled blankets
on such a hot sticky night
maybe neither
nude under a blue sheet
try to sleep

don't want him to kiss me
his lips are soft
his brown skin is smooth
don't want to twist to face him
his body is strong & gentle
the insides of my body turn
slowly so do I
still my lips touch
our eyes
in darkness
bodies beneath the sheets
I turn away
think of you
elsewhere

∽

second skin

fingers one by one placed carefully
around edges of memory

smell presence in dream
see presents around neck
mementoes of a past
cauldron stewing in my head
sleep with this stir
& stir
this a ghost of the past
attractive presence in the present
slip off my skirt
pull my sweater over head
throw it drunkenly on the floor
in the dusty corner
come
devour me whole
instead
I wrap my undershirt & tights
taut like a second skin
around me &
confusion
crush the edges of this memory

entwined

hazy light dim in London
I've just finished a glass of brandy
you are in the bath reading
my mother next door feels sorry for herself
wants to return to Canada probably cried herself to sleep
I step into your room double bed on the floor
covers folded back. I see a tiny blue flame
flicker hear a soft hiss from the gas fire
I undress jump into bed light still on
as you enter the room close the door
remove your long white terrycloth housecoat
& crawl in beside me. you shut the light
wind the clock in darkness & reach over
curl around me. a seahorse. soft body
nudges into mine. I have never felt the erect nipples
of another woman's breasts on my back
before. your hands dance on the front of my body
my breasts. my sides. down my thighs. you
wrap your finger loosely around the curls
of my hair. I turn & face you kiss
my forehead. I pull my knees to my chest you
wrap your legs around my body cradle me
as though I've taken a bad fall.
our bodies twist & tangle.
as you undressed tonight I thought
what a beautiful pear-shaped body you have. yes
I remember you.
when I phoned & asked
how would we recognize each other
at the airport
you laughed.

butterfly

flushed cheeks blush colour
surface warm
electric feelings between two people ignite
she was my friend
a mind like the path a butterfly flies
stops long enough to inhale the sweetness of the flower
then flutters on to the next
we danced & drank joy
filled bodies rooms where thought bounced
off walls our minds crickets sang at night
lay our heads quietly on white theologians' pillows
& we were

now in the present present
skin soaks up smells swells
the caress of a hand powerful
as though never before touched
crippled sexuality blossoms with silence
& absence fear gone replaced by desire
the sunday mid-afternoon nap turns
from an erotic dream into a deep pool of slow love
making we are drawn into our streams from which we draw
the deliciousness of desire rainbow swirls of colour
& taste bright lights of intimacy

mouthful

you nibble cajole awaken aliven chew tease nibble again my
nipple my nipples in your mouth alive awaken from the nest
beneath bra & soft cotton t-shirt alert to your fingertips tongue
lips suck forward feel the energy rise to chest toss & turn around
inside the body swirling toe to fingertips stop look into my eyes
smile dip back down again knead chew with teeth lips the cyprine
between mine secretes slowly feel the sweat breaks over our bodies
you say still you cup my breasts in both hands gently gently you
sway your hair over my long body sweep it clean across borders
we cross daily

your hand brushes my skin as fingers running through hot
summer sand to my thigh & tease the curls between my legs lift
cleft writhe in desire again that look upwards at me face between
my legs that smile you blow coolly then your tongue a feather
drifts over me & desire tidal waves over the edges & another &
yet another until the full moon is in my belly being licked stroked
the stars as bright as on a moonless night all sound ceases except
for the explosion of meteors throughout my body

cyprine — *from Nicole Brossard's* Under Tongue. *Female sexual
secretion. From the French* cyprine *[fr. GK Cyprus, birth place of
Aphrodite]*.

no visual scars

Pain reaches the heart with electrical speed,
but truth *moves to the heart as slowly as a glacier.*

— Barbara Kingsolver, from *Animal Dreams*

addict

i

I am dirty scum scavenge money to buy
my weakness need to escape life fills
my veins squeeze out blood screams black
train tracks up & down between my toes my thin
body aches not just arms crave pain feel it soaked
in good heroin & heroine white shit I eat feed into
anyway possible don't let anyone listen hooked
on it hard stuff good stuff something fixed inside
inside my head black vein white coke smack my lips
from hunger is it a deprivation of what?
on an edge the shiny razor edge no matter
which way I'll fall over into
off off off of

ii

clenched fist jab my elbow into gut
push & push strike the vein a bubble
of blood on my arm good hit there it is
a rush throb inside my bruised heart
see it fill with black ink what's in there
that makes me hurt so much this
will kill it yeah come on kick it
over   here it goes   oh my god
oh my god my heart my heart so fast
come on baby slow down come on I can't

Deanna

can barely speak
only three
bare naked at night
cute shiny bum
in the bath
in her bed
where she is not safe

this is for you
the child within that fears
the night
dark blanket that covers
but offers no comfort

she clutches Cabbage Patch dolls
stutters reaching for words
she hasn't yet learned
what happens to her
nightly or weekly
even if it happens only weekly
it adds up
to a life
full of night terror
what fucking clichés left
for her to hear
when she finally has an ear

her mother hears him taking a shower
four in the morning
while she pretends to sleep
what is his reason for these
late night rapes
of their daughter?

I remember holding her
in the playground
screaming NO together
at the top of our lungs
so at night when daddy hurt her
she too could say No
she hasn't been on this earth long
enough to even know
yes or no
when someone touches her
in her sleep
only knows the hurt
we screamed loud together
we screamed long
both collapsing in laughter
everyone watching us
knowing the seriousness
of the simple word

yes Deanna I think of you
today
your parents' wedding
a secret ceremony
in the cold of dead winter
years after you & your brother were born
secrets
all of them
all your life
how long will you have
to hold on to this one?

up against the wall

it's time again to confront the dark
this isn't about scampering rabbits
or blooming tulips at Easter
she must walk straight into the forest
the event: his birthday next week
& all she thinks about is
how she wakes from her own screaming
this is the kind of poem mothers hate
to hear about restless, disturbing sleep
night after night
she wraps her flannel quilt to her chin
like the proverbial child until
he enters the shadows   once again
places his body over hers
a mask hovers above her face breathing
motionless stares bright white sound
his face burns into her
he appears old & wrinkled behind money signs
she leaps from her sleep
& is screaming
as though a gun were pointed at her head
smashes her fingernails up against the wall
twisted backwards blood rushes
screaming
the cry of her own voice wakes her
up against the wall
bloody hands
sweaty & frenzied who is there?
who is it that smothers just by reaching
inside her head

she walks to the washroom
fills the basin with cold water

what can she possibly say on his birthday card?
what gift is appropriate now?

the thief

it's not the thief who crouched at the end of the bed
to be afraid of anymore
it's the one who hides in the mind & jumps out
from behind closed doors who haunts
the one who picked deep into his nose
then wiped the blood on arms
who smudged soiled underwear on the body
who with the friend molested
& looked through peepholes
who crashed in on baths
& wandered in to sleep when he felt like it
this is the thief to fear
isn't the one that crouched
at the end of the bed
the symbol for all the others still lurking
inside the bones?

transparent skin

look inside all you see is a moonless dark so thick it could be
sliced with a hand. chopped in half the seams would instantly sew
themselves back together. you hate this feeling hides & pounces
when you're unaware. the hidden agenda. you want the tears to
stop. fears to stop. to sleep soundly straight through a night. so
in turmoil no one understands, you want them to know you've
spent your entire portion of pain & you're only 23. you think of
the men who instilled the fear to make you act accordingly
submissive & now you have anger heaped onto the fear &
sadness. this helplessness having no control over your body with
its transparent skin.

scared peace

you stare at the ceiling night after night sleep all day sometimes
for days in scared peace the world you seep into rest like a child
your eyelids flutter softly shhh in dream a picture you'll never see
unless a photo is snapped eating chocolate bars, french fries,
suckling on cigarettes smoke fills your eyes a burning haze you
walk through at night drink beer after beer when finally you're
convinced to come out so drunk when we return yet can't sleep
you pace like Napoleon holding yourself frozen cell state keyless
prison I ask to gently wipe your tears scream down your pale
face but no your hand goes up to shield the black mascara bars
nobody has the tools to cut through the barbed wire you're
cradled in

minimum security

to Terry

neither of us has been here before. neither of us knows Terry very
well. we stand in line & I glance up & down the hallway. my eyes
fix on a woman. in black leather pants & a leather jacket. chains
around her waist. chews gum.

I am pushed through tall metal gates. clank. a guard sits behind a
metal desk. name. relationship to prisoner. sign here. next. Doug
follows me.

no — you go with him. you — come with me.

I watch Doug follow the guard through metal gates then out of
sight. another guard escorts me down a cement-block corridor
past a smoky room with people & a cigarette machine. I hear the
guard's heels click against the shiny tiled floor.

wait here.

I am alone in the corridor in front of a door with a sign *native
clan.* I hope they bring Doug back. at least I wore the right
clothing. faded jeans & jean jacket blond hair covered with a
black bandana. beaded moccasins. I was told to dress in dark
colours so I wouldn't feel out of place.

the door opens. the biker woman comes out buttoning up her
blouse quickly. two white women stand in the room, both young
— no more than 25 — close together. they look like friends. one
fat the other thin. both wear mustard-coloured smocks. little
girlish. they belong behind a counter in a drugstore or in a

hospital for elderly people. the fat woman's eyes are circled with blue eyeliner. a cat. as I enter the room her right hand struggles into a transparent surgical glove.

have you been here before? asks the thin one. no. sign this form. this is so we can search you. oh. the paper asks for the prisoner's name & my name. I can't remember Terry's last name. the form says if I don't want to sign I won't see the prisoner.

take off your clothes. leave on your underwear.

the thin woman searches my wallet & jewellery. asks if my flat ring or solid pendant open. the other searches the cavities & crevices of my body. in my ear around the cartilage. tilts her head to look up my nose. pulls my eyelids up. runs her finger along my gums & under my tongue. between my toes. slips her hand under my bra & slides her rubber glove along my sweaty body.

lie on the table.

this is not a doctor's office table. it is a round kitchen table. the native clan might have had a few good card games around it. the thin woman sits down crosses her legs & unwraps a piece of bubblegum. she reads the comic & snickers aloud. the table is cold against my back. the light casts an immense shadow on the white wall as the large woman approaches.

relax.

the woman slides two fingers underneath my panties & inside of me. I jump. she does this many times a day. I try to look into her eyes. make a human connection.

get dressed.

the two women stand staring at me as I dress. it stings between my legs & I want to put my hand down there to soothe the pain. my jewellery & wallet are returned to me. I button my shirt as I leave the room. my hands shake as I place the rings back on my fingers.

go to your right up the hall.

I walk into a large, smoky cafeteria where human warmth embraces me. talking & laughter. the room is filled with young men in dark green pants & light blue t-shirts. I look for Terry & am startled to see him in prison garb, already with Doug. I settle myself in silence on an orange chair at the square institutional table. we'll now attempt to reach across the void in which we're caught.

Belfast

two wee girls
were playing tig near a car...

how many countries would you say
are worth their scattered fingers?
  — Desmond Egan

    red iron prison gates 15 feet high block off side streets from main ones. gates with bent toe claw prongs for peaks. once your bag & body have been frisked you're in & you're not leaving for awhile. makes shopping downtown unforgettable. a rat's nest of barbed wire circles parking lots rooftops guards against people climbing over to place, to set a bomb off inside a car, a bookstore, shopping plaza. all vehicles stopped at barricades inside the main streets. make time for the British soldiers to look us over. search us through. people here must leave home sooner to arrive on time. police in blue trench coats backcatcher padded vests over top. black long leather gloves boots. guards everywhere search for the unfound bomb loaded guns & rifles pointed ready at you. undercoats. overcoats. closet thoughts. unnerving. reminds me of being in Poland. but this is by choice the way these people live?

    signs posted DO NOT PARK YOUR CAR AGAINST THIS GATE. a friend of Shirley's did by accident police exploded the car. just in case. still where I sit in this restaurant eat chips & vinegar quench my fear Irish girls after school in maroon uniforms & white blouses hang over seats swoon over local boyos' school crests in the next booth. pass around one or two cigarettes among them. a middle-aged woman sits sips her cup of white tea & pulls slowly on her smoke. busses go & come on schedule in front of the cafe.

taxis. cars. groups of boys pass by in uniforms. whose side are they on? will they hoist me for money in a narrow alleyway? crumbling remnants of buildings. splattering of blood on falling brick walls POST NO BILLS the sign says. graffiti rampant just like the scarred youth who wrote it. stopped a woman on the street to ask where the historic sites were. *they've all been destroyed by the 'troubles' haven't they?* the troubles she calls this war zone city.

Valentine's Day. free pink cake in the restaurant today. a perfect day for a bombing. a day to extend your love. double fear of being pulled over by police for just being here in the wrong store at the wrong time, wrong street, wrong bus. sorry, wrong place to be. step on a streetgrate imagine the whole street up in flames. no public benches to wait for a bus or train only directions what to do if you spot an unidentified lone package or bag. this is the first country where a stranger asked my religion before my name.

the ring

I fiddle with my gold ring take it off & look
scratch marks from Eaton's meat
department local 584 downtown store slinging pork
side ribs onto a wooden chopping block
cleaver in hand customers lean on metal meat case
waiting for their pink numbers to be called
amazed a tiny woman could be so fierce
with such a blade blood
liver on my hands smells of fresh fish in the
glass cooler next to chicken necks my hands my hands
I wash them 20 times a day in a metal
bucket beside the counter on the floor wipe
them on my white uniform hear bones
sawed in the back on a tablesaw leave the meat
a 20-minute break ride up the escalator
fifth floor through children's clothes
in the cafeteria choose a cinnamon bun & tea
sit at tables pushed together bosses
with blue tags & regular employees like me
nurses cap pinned in place on my head
get stopped in the store where's the first aid room?
no, I work with meat fiddle with my ring
as I talk over coffee about trips to Mexico, Las Vegas
25 years at Eaton's is like the first year
only repeated 25 times no wonder they escape
yearly to a new exotic place
you gave me this ring when I began working here
did I ever say thank you?

2:30 a.m.

the hour of death
of piercing babies' cries
of the most intense orgasms
of watching the stillness of the dark
calm night
the time death confronts
what if we had only 24 more hours
who would we phone?
what book would we read?
what records would we listen to?
at this hour
we confront such possibilities
because we can see no end
to the state we're in
that last breath, gasp, grasp of hand

I asked my father the doctor
had he ever witnessed
the final breath of a patient
like in the movies?
I only remember him saying yes
& then sharp silence
no mention of feelings

the passing
passage from this world to that
in ceremony & pomp
or solemness & fear
knowing at funerals often the soul of the dead
is in the room watching
to see who attended

yet at 2:30 a.m.
thoughts run like rats
scratch my brain
so big too big to wrestle to death
I rise
to write

plaster of paris

after Donald Brittain

there is never anything new about horror
even with the mention of Auschweitz Dauchau or Belsen
but as the black & white film reel turns
that time slowly burns & re-turns
we ignore those days these days
in the comfort of homes
watch the glamour of crimes against humanity trials
everybody yet nobody would be shocked if it recurred

the woman on the screen
descends the tour bus stairs 1965
twenty years after *The War*
the commentator asks why she returns
she is alive & the barbed wire
no longer entangles her life
but the blue numbers braided on her arm
won't let go

the German guide announces that everyone
Germans & Jews alike
will take their horrible place in history

my womb aches from the plaster of paris
they poured inside the women

there's a whole lot of people dying tonight
from the disease of conceit — Bob Dylan

want to reach over open your eyes
so bright used to be
so excitable energetic
you hold back
the embrace wooden
though the world will only heal
with affection
people afraid
gossip
aware every time we speak
many people sit with us in conversation
so aware words paralysed in lungs
my heart still hoping for connection
the body as house the doorstep
not even invited in
is it age that makes us callous
or cautious in conversation
that breeds contempt?
people die
of this disease
called conceit
will you too?

from destination to destiny

dream
a backdrop
where we converse with the dead
gain understanding as to why
we must endure this labyrinthine inferno

the smouldering from the nazi ovens
stank of the wickedness of ignorance
& intolerance fed with bodies
that had no moment to question
what bound flesh to spirit

in my *baba's* house the living & dead
were on speaking terms
she cursed to a mother long gone
for no help during hardship
thanked the air when guidance came

tears coagulate with pain
create a paste of anger & defiance

there is such a thing as evil
we are not born with the knowledge
but all have been taught what it is
we must dream & walk with the spirits
listen or we will be responsible for perishing
in compliance

December 1989

the smell of fresh human blood
broken neck where the bullet enters her spine
head clunks on the desk
drains of blood
the soul drifts away & above
to watch the next woman being aimed at
hands over ears, eyes closed tight
see no evil hear no evil
surrounds & binds us to our terror
14 women chosen
target practise

mourn in candlelight vigil
people keen & wail
drums pound blood red
rage at being the bull's-eye
fat wallets roam porn clubs
beer bellies skinny necks & large heads
will have to move over
walk beside those who appear to have nothing
no division: us & them
eliminate the fear of difference of others
flowers of fear bloom with money
love: no bank loans for that

evil binds us to our terror
binds us to fear binds us
to evil
now, now
we must liberate ourselves

no visual scars

tired sometimes of the pain moving to pleasure. only a hop from one word to another yet the step-in-mind miles from where the feet are. the private rooms of the heart we get locked into & out of no privacy to see beyond always trapped behind a door. go on — open it. we open up musty drawers of hidden things long ago forgotten circumvented circled around side stepped towards the house body the torturous nights of tears curled away. doors slam & you know it will begin again. it's those damn doors we hear. we remember.

re-membering parts of the body. gluing back what limbs have come unstuck there are no visual scars. lines crisscross beneath flesh a web woven inside tangles up with tendons blood from head to toe the goal to keep breathing make sense of the pounding of our brains. try. it is the trying that saves us moves us into new strength.

portraits of pregnant women

The history of anyone must be a long one.

— Gertrude Stein

The history of anyone must be a long one & a pregnant one. Large, emotional, growing, always giving birth to new ideas, gifts, circumstances. We all began the same way. Let us be introduced to Ruby, Ramona, Roberta, Felicity, & Dea. There will be others & you'll hear their birth tales too.

Felicity

Feliz — happiness yes she is incarnate at the moment she knows she's conceived. So many miles from her own truth something acting upon her pleases. No control — finally she can relinquish that; tired of always being. Out of control now gaining weight changing bra sizes week after week her long honey-coloured hair once silky feels sticky after washing. Could only eat toast for months & once she ate a food couldn't manage to swallow it again. Coffee made her nauseous. Sleeping an hour at work everyday — set up a cot in a back office out of view. A promotion didn't materialize good a time as any to become pregnant. Ramification for this Felicity? For this, *felicitations!* Does she know who she is? What are her interests & desires? She didn't know before conception, when will she know? A child bearing a child some would say. Pregnancy all encompassing, to the point of forgetting, or giving up knowing who you are? Too far. Giving your child the gift of a parent who doesn't know her true desires. That's no gift to openly embrace a newborn with. Giving in order to receive. Except when the receiver doesn't care or worse, doesn't notice. Spent weeks walking along the Thames discussing the pros & cons of pregnancy. Lists written in eyeliner pencil on the back of a torn bill. She'd had an abortion & never sorted it through to be pregnant again meant the same mind twisting. False alarm. Two months later the bell was ringing for her. Her wish to be pregnant. Used birth control but so strong a desire all control was lost. To cleanse, absolve herself of old wounds. Correct her errors. No more guilt or shame. This time she would have a child.

Happiness like true pain comes like medicine to those in prison. It sustains & strengthens you.

Ruby

Ruby red. Wrestles with the miracle marvels at her daughter, a doctor's word defied. Ruby was told she would never radiate with child so when she was nauseous that week in April she thought she had flu. Baked potatoes for the first three months she shone like a gem as she stitched her baby's quilt before birth. Afraid her foetus wasn't active enough, because of her age she volunteered for foetal monitoring, kicks & nudges. She was going to be induced but at that thought the baby appeared. Her dear one now is the most calm, felicitous, agreeable infant parents could ever ask for.

The first day of life Ruby & precious huddled together in their hospital bed while photographs of the birth were shown. Ruby became angry because the series wasn't to be seen. Powerful, amazonian clenching of hands, bearing down; wildness of long hair mixed with sweat, grunting & screaming almost audible blood streaming down insides of thighs, hair mixed with sweat, blood with force, green sanitized fabric covered all parts except vagina, thighs & legs opened wide for the light to touch the child's crown, sucked into this whirlwind. The newborn in Ruby's arms later, both mother & daughter completely sterilized in only the North American fashion — white & pure. Smiling at the camera. Blue bags beneath Ruby's eyes, yet strength behind the smile saying I did it & the miracle child is here. No eating of placenta for this duo.

Six months later Ruby waits in her doctor's office for a referral to a gyn/ob. The one at the birth sewed her tear up so tight said, *I'll put an extra stitch in for the husband* sex is now physically impossible. She was told she'd *loosen up* eventually. Now she has to be sliced open again & re-stitched because this helpful stand-in doctor was overzealous. Malpractice? No comment. You had a child? her doctor asks. Yes. It's not physically possible. Yes. It is & it was.

The miracle child with red shoes will click her heels & dance through storms.

Ramona

First born child of her family. Night & day see her from my kitchen window rush in & out, in & out car to house her door next to ours. Always on the go. Always there. Over-functioning, the new pop-psych word. Her first child cried & cried, we almost called the Children's Aid. What was(n't) being done for this infant. The girl is just feisty & self-assured, until the diabetes hit a few months ago. Grandma called in from Squamish, kept the house humming until a semblance of normalcy was reached. Normalcy, what's that with a baby? Ramona always takes care of business, total control. She is trapped by her own need for chaos & crisis — the only level she knows how to function at, anything less for her is not really living. Until the day of her second child's birth & she needed all the over-functioning she could muster. Christmas Day: food, laughter, gifts, contractions, & pictionary. Until the contractions came too close & strong & she threw down her pencil in aggravation because she couldn't decipher her partner's clues & began to give birth. In the car rushed to hospital 45 minute labor & back at home within five hours.

Ramona dedicated Ramona tries to be Mother to all — doing for everybody. Staying in town? Stay with Ramona. Have an illness? Call Ramona. It's too bad for her that she's always there. Disease & unease surround her. Skin withers with stretching movements of being a mom. Her spirit now like a holocaust victim: trapped inside a shrinking body, hollowed eyes, sunken cheek bones, boney knees & hands, baby at a shrivelling breast. She takes another night class, teaches one, works a weekly 12-hour shift, mothers a daughter with diabetes & a nine-month old son, volunteers at the cancer society, tries to be a wife & a friend.

Maybe she'll have 20 seconds to herself. Is this what motherhood is? Chaos, such a lonely & intimate friend of those with heaviness in their hearts. No one is ever proud of their pain. But some try so desperately to pretend they have none they wear it like a smock. Always a cover. Aching loneliness. A voice which hardly ever reaches out spirals inward to create a labyrinth of martyrdom.

Is this motherhood?

Roberta

for Harlan

Ruby red lipstick at every glance this woman has. Six months as
this is written pregnant & counting. She bops on her bike
around the city covering miles rarely contemplated in a car.
Effervescent without coffee, gave up long, slender cigarettes a few
years back quite delicious gave up the company of wine quaffing
& puffing on a long smoke in between nail polished fingertips
gave up sitting in Parisian or Spanish cafes, the bodegas of
Vancouver. Gave that up to give life. All drugs put aside for a
fraction of a lifetime to give the kid a clean start. Then we hear of
dioxins in mother's breast milk. Is the unborn ever safe? Her belly
swells, stretch marks do exist & nightly she reads to her foetus,
ball of cells she affectionately calls *Ballo-O* while rubbing coconut
cream on her belly. Stories & poetry to comfort mother-to-be &
child-to-be-mothered. An aversion to violence grows in propor-
tion to new-found quietness she saw a war film & left queasy &
unbalanced. She looked so un-pregnant that day. Pooling her
tears for certain nights picks up the phone to talk a thick buoyant
circle of friends surrounds. Not a wrinkle on her brow, or a new
grey hair on her head. Instead she lengthens it to grow in its
natural colour. Her humour never faltering as she simulates birth
pulling her turtleneck sweater slowly over head — first the loose
woolen neck of sweater: before labour; next the sight of her hair
through the neck: the crowning; finally her resplendently smiling
face appears: the birth.

Now just days before the end of the nine months. She's given up the bike in place a pair of sturdy legs she walks everywhere. Vulnerability as close to the surface as blood is to her ruby cheeks glow in the light of pregnancy. Tears at the drop of an insensitive comment. She has cocooned herself & home for the newness.

Witnessing not only the birth of a child, but the birth of a parent, a woman.

Dea

Where are you tonight? In your Tucson home where the cactus roam & the wind carries howling baby cries to meet you now you have two. I could hardly believe when we came back from our walk in Winnipeg that a three-year old yelling *mommy, mommy* was running to greet you. You — a mommy? Now again, a child. I don't even recall this one's name. You once thought you were pregnant when we were in athletic training — I skipped school to join you at the pregnancy testing clinic. Negative results but enough fear of the possibility to last a lifetime. If you were with that mad scientist now? Would you be any sadder? Invisible years of changing diapers, wearing ruby red fluff-ball slippers Beatles on the CD player — the modern day mom. Has that world swallowed you whole? Not a peep since your second crowned his head in your hands. Arduous thankless time glides by day by day & you wonder what it was you accomplished — the reward of seeing a sick child smile? Have you read a book or seen a film lately? What is your life like now with two at your feet — one must be in school. Wow & in America? Your children are Yanks — even in all your wildest dreams in your tiny basement bedroom where Ian Drury & Tom Waits blasted did you ever imagine your children would be pledging allegiance to the U.S. government? I wish you well mom. Fellow former athlete who's doing the best with what you've been given & on the path you've cut through with what you've chosen. I hope I see you before your children graduate.

Do you really make them pledge their allegiance?

Alexandra

Hopes, prayers, expectations, scenarios of conception. What if you're given only 14 days to prepare to be parents? No bodily changes, no psychological nine month prep time, only papers to sign & clearing your conscience enough to know that this is *really* what you want. Two felicitous professors, stable income, a paid-off house in the suburbs, white, musical, well-travelled. She's had every test, tipped her uterus this way & that during intercourse. Had basal thermometers up her bum, in her vagina, beneath her tongue & armpit. He's been in cubicles ejaculating to four walls with a microscope waiting behind closed doors to examine his virility. She's had a laporoscopy, he's had children with another woman & yet they cannot conceive. Model parents? From the outside anyway. A child is born Thanksgiving Day. They are called three days before — the chosen parents from photographs of 20 couples. After the birth, the biological mother has ten days to retract her offer. The Chosen Ones. The mother waits until the very last day to hand over her creation. In trust for the next 18 years when the child will probably go looking for his birth parents. Now they're the same as any other mom & dad: sleepless nights, hungry & cranky both parents & child. Isolation being with an infant every hour of every day. When will the baby be exhausted enough to flop? Hope, pray, expect just one night, maybe tonight he'll sleep through.

Babies come to us in mysterious ways.

Louise

A lesbian for many years in academia wants desperately to have a child. With her various lovers she's talked about the procedure, but none are willing to be co-moms. Finally word filters through the infamous pipeline Louise has met a man & is happier than she's been forever. We meet in Safeway one evening & she tells me of a trip to the doctor's because she's been vaginally bleeding. The doctor asks if she's er, a virgin at 38. No, but this is the first man she's slept with for ten years & that might be the reason she's so tight. Embarrassed but reassured things will loosen up she tells me the story. Next thing we know we're all going to be aunts & uncles to her & Paul's baby. They are as shocked as all of us going out for six months, but ready as ever to begin. Again. Her political friends can't quite make all of this out. First with men, then with women, back with a man, & now with child?

The womb is no longer in place of the brain.

milk of the mother born

milk of the mother born of milk
& soured when not satisfied in adult existence
our lips suck on nipples at least once in a lifetime
no denying whatever the orientation
nipples & lips have the same skin
blood rushes to their surface to expand & beckon
milk pushes forward just as blood
did to create babes now suckle at the breast
bees at flowers draw out nectar
the sun settles into pores
a kiss on the lips
of words
the surface of milkiness
skin in a cool mountain morning
the sun unpretentiously walks
over mountaintops milk streams slowly in
as the morning begins

every mother is the daughter of a daughter who has not been mothered

mum's the word   did you hear that
ma'am
mom
mum
a daughter perhaps your daughter
a mother
my mother
grandmother
all daughters of mothers who were daughters
not mothered

muuuum come & tuck us in

hear the echoes bounce off three flights of stairs
she's too tired to climb
kiss good night
on occasion
we would yell & yell
finally fall silent to dream
forget her absence in the morning

to mum: to go silent & act
as a mummer
one who wears masks & disguises; an actor

how do women know how to be mothers?
but to mum they know   camouflage their inadequacies
in learning my role as woman, as nurturer

72

my first child was you
my mother

her double-jointed rounded thumbs point back at herself
her wide laugh
sometimes nervous
among men
leans forward gesticulates to make a point
hands poised midair
trying to hold   meaning
she grasped for a nanosecond

the woman who was her mother
is her today
to me as a mother what she gave she gave
from her own small stash of child strength

a steel bar
runs up our backs
holds us upstraight
this was the embrace our mothers offered

the women who took care of us
their need for acceptance & nurturance
so great
as daughters we mothered

from tormenting silence the humiliated are born
mummified words unravel from wounds
I've rolled away the stone

in the molecules of darkness
stories are carried
we grope for faces
to recognize at the light switch
finally painful silence is quietened by speech

to stop mothering my mother
will be truly taking care

The title was taken from an article, *Covert Incest in Women's Lives: Dynamics and Directions For Healing,* by N.D. Hyde.

the women's (dressing) room

bums all widths crinkles & wrinkles white & red stretch marks if put end to end would stretch for miles in any direction. secrets hide in pockets of cellulite, in thighs, in arms & breasts. the aureoles chocolate brown, cream-coloured, pinkish, purple as we undress in our corners stuff our clothing into lockers & pin the key to bathing suits. the safety of this room for these few moments. little girls gape at women's bodies, wondering will theirs be like that one day. I remember thinking it. one little girl exclaims *look her hair 'down there' is red too!* a learning place. in the shower a woman shaves her upper thighs to have the perfect triangle of pubic hair. walking naked, feeling relaxed, even if someone in curiosity gawks, shoulders shrug & pass to the sauna to lounge where sweat bursts pores open in nakedness. safety. yes. for a few moments. no fear of taking our clothes off, that a stranger *(read male)* may see us. even in front of our windows at night we fear someone *(read male)* may be watching. or if we live alone, someone *(ditto)* might break in & we all know the rest. here women of all shapes & sizes native, chinese, japanese, irish, philopena, ukrainian, vietnamese, chubby, tall, big-bosomed, with the same anatomical parts: vagina, pubic hair, breasts, a face, arms, legs, thighs, toes, feet, hands, hair of varying lengths, shades & styles. are we all to be syphoned into one mold? a large italian woman in the shower twists her right foot to shave away pubic hair creeping down her thighs. we don't need to slice & shave our true selves away. we can walk into the public pool strong, varying proportioned with ideas & feelings unique instead of the one dimensional cut-out pictures so many women buy & squeeze ourselves into.

the hairdresser

same treatment all of us. arrive a quarter hour late & leave three
later hair newly styled in between a greek coffee, a cigarette or
two a roach if you're in the mood & wine if not, you catch up on
each other's lives in her kitchen facing a full-length mirror her
fingers run through hair you talk rarely face her discuss her trip to
Greece yours to Montreal selling mud make-up being on welfare
you're on welfare she's on welfare next visit you're not she's not
talk about a $10 tip on a $12 haircut Robin the name of a bird
heard stepping into her apartment. & left. dreams, sculptures,
masks, peach-coloured living room a toilet that never flushes she
always looks different her hair shorter or longer than the last & of
course her child if you're there over lunch she makes it for him or
after 3:30 the tv with cartoons & his friends circled around it she
never flusters or so it seems anger appears occasionally & her
brothers too the goddess the mother the whore she extends
beyond all those male definitions of woman of who she is try to
capture an essence precious & honest there she is looking at you
in the mirror scissors in hand laughing

Remember It Well

Christmas Day. A birth day. You remember it well. Leisurely breakfast, orange juice, croissants & jam. Both of you wearing housecoats & slippers. Slide into the living room leaving the dishes for later & open your gifts. Calendars. Cake. Tea cup. Chocolates. Books. Records. Jewellery. Scuba diving lessons. Wrapping paper & bows strewn all over. You have three hours before dinner so you hop up the stairs back to bed. Under the lightness & joy of the feather quilt & the thrill of someone's birth day you make love.

Two weeks later a pain in your left ovary. Afraid another cyst is forming you phone the medical clinic. They can see you tomorrow.

Go to the accountant's to prepare your income tax & she tells you of her recent pregnancy. You tell her your period is five days late — not really too unusual especially after an overseas trip. But the pain in the left ovary. She said sounds like pregnancy pain. She mentions a home testing kit, $13 & you find out right away if you are or not. You don't want to know right now, in the middle of sorting out how much in debt you are.

After the meeting you do buy the kit. The student pharmacist tells you he's used one, er, that he was once in a predicament where his friend used one & thought it was very reliable. As you pay he says, *I don't know what result you're looking for, but good luck.* Doesn't the look on your face give you away?

You wait until morning to pee into the plastic cup. Draw a bath. Like an amateur chemist you pour the urine into the small vial, shake it up, pour it through the tiny filter & jump into the embracing warmth of the bath water.

You dry yourself off, no peeking before you're ready. Some part of you already knows. Already. Knows. You've heard women who were pregnant say, somehow they knew.

Then, the pink of the filter, you are pregnant.

At the doctor's appointment in the morning your home results are confirmed. Perhaps the pain in your left ovary is a sign of an ectopic pregnancy. A tubal implantation. Perhaps not. Just your hormones going wacko. The doctor asks you what you are going to do; that is the beginning of the tears. A T.A. the doctor tells the receptionist so she can give you a referral to a gynecologist. T.A. Therapeutic Abortion. Again the water from your eyes. Blinking it back. Reaching for a kleenex to blow your running nose. This can't really be happening. Not to you. Why? pounds against the sides of your brain. From the left to the right. *Why me? Why me?* The pain surges to your throat. The memory of having no control yet so much emotion. Nothing tangible but the tears. Cells divide inside your body as the tears fall.

The heavy, heavy feeling of knowing you are pregnant. A foetus. Grows inside. Perhaps not yet the size of the eraser on the end of a pencil. Maybe only the size of the tip of a wick on an unlit candle. But it exists. In its own form. There inside.

Whose choice is this?

A friend phones. You tell her. She is surprised & happy, you explain you don't want to be pregnant. Twice the phone rings & the incident repeats itself. You don't tell your friend who has fought for four months to keep her premature baby alive. Or your friend who is pregnant or the one who wants to be.

An invisible line is drawn directly between your brain & womb every time your mind is not occupied. The trajectory direct from heart to head. The longest journey.

You never wonder if it is male or female. Blood stockpiling. Swooshing around. To you, it is no larger than the speck at the end of this sentence you will live with for the rest of your life.

Choice isn't a big enough word for the decision a woman makes when she chooses not to be pregnant any longer. The decision will live forever with you in your body.

So you gaze at the purple & white roses & magenta heather sitting quietly on your desk with you & your decision. The fragrance so complex & strong. The colours deep & soothing.

You know, no person can kill a soul.